Gary the Go-Cart
Wind Blows

Written by BB Denson

Illustrated by Sidnei Marques

Desideramus Publishing - Houston, TX

Gary was a go-cart. Gary loved to go fast.
Flying downhill, Gary always had a blast.
Faster and faster and faster he'd go,
no matter the weather, no matter the snow.

Gary was happy – happy as could be,
zipping downhill, his heart filled with glee.

Gary loved going downhill. Downhill he went fast.
But Gary had a problem he could not get past.

Gary liked to do for others. He was rarely waylaid.
He'd like to earn a living. He'd like to be paid.

Gary would watch, day in and day out,
cars and trucks delivering all about.

How they made those deliveries

was one of life's big mysteries.

What is the problem? Why can't he do this task?
What is it that stops him, what is it you ask?

Well, he needed to go uphill. Gravity pulled him down.
He needed power to go uphill and then to get around.

"I want to go far, I want to go fast.
I don't want to be slow like go-carts from the past."

What would make his heart sing?
What'd give this go-cart wing?
Where to ask and find answers?
Who knew lots of things?
Professors, tap dancers,
news anchors or kings?

News anchors he thought.

They knew lots of things.

Enlightenment he sought.

Shall we see what that brings?

He turned on the TV.

He learned all he could.

He saw lots of bickering and watched for the good.

Gary noticed the Greenies
each night in the news.
How smart looked those
Greenies.
They'd know what to do.

Gary went to the Greenies.
He proffered his quest.
For solutions, dear Greenies.
This is my request.

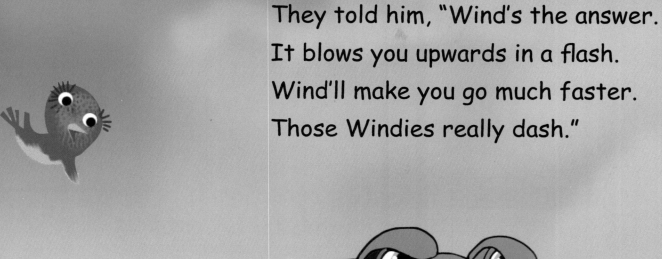

They told him, "Wind's the answer.
It blows you upwards in a flash.
Wind'll make you go much faster.
Those Windies really dash."

"See the pinwheels spin when it's windy.
The spinning runs them fast!
Their pinwheels are so dandy.
Those Windies have a blast."

So, he went to the land of the Windies.
He could not believe his eyes.
He found them sitting quite still.
It was such a surprise.

Why were they not moving?
Why not having a blast?
Why were they just sitting there?
Why at long, long last?

Seems the wind only works, when and where it wants to be.
When the wind isn't blowing, those Windies are up a tree.

See, the wind blows in blasts. Between each blast it's
slow. For the pinwheels to work, they need that wind to
blow.

Gary thought about what he'd heard,
then a movement caught his eye.
Why, it was birds! And they were racing by!

He stopped a birdie and asked her,
"Why are you rushing away?
What is the hurry? Why do you not stay?"

The Birdie said,
"Those pinwheels may be pretty, those pinwheels may look good.
It is truly a pity, that they are hard as wood."

"Those pinwheels scare us birds, those pinwheels make us flee.
Those pinwheels hurt us birds, near them we cannot be."

Then the birdie whispered to Gary
that he ought to look at gas.
She said that if he had it, she knew he could go fast.

"Gas?" thought Gary. "Should I perhaps be wary?"
"I try to be clever. I try to be smart.
Let's think this thing through, right from the very start."

"With gas can I go up the hills?
With gas, can I work?
With gas can I pay my bills
And not end up berserk?"

"Is there gas when I need it? Is there gas when wind's not blown? Yes! There is gas when I need it! And my budget won't groan!"

"There is gas when winds don't blow, and when there's no sunshine. There is gas for me uphill to go. Perhaps this will all be fine!"

"Maybe gas is the answer. With gas I can go fast! Seems that gas is always there. Uphill to go at last!"

"Now with gas, I zoom the hills.
With gas, I get things done.
Now with gas, I pay my bills.
With gas, uphill I run!"

Now Gary spends his days
going uphill and down.
Never a harsh word
and never a frown.

Now Gary makes deliveries. He likes getting things done.

His life is free of miseries. His life is full of fun.

Uphill is not a burden. Uphill is now a blast.

"With gas I can go far! With gas I can go fast!

I am no longer slow like go-carts from the past!"

Gary was happy. Happy as could be.

Uphill and down, his heart filled with glee.

Desideramus Publishing
Houston, TX
Desideramus.com

For information about custom editions, special sales and premium or corporate purchases, please contact Desideramus Publishing.

CPSIA information can be obtained at www.ICGtesting.com
Printed in the USA
LVIW01n1103050616
491308LV00013B/69